For Jack Foley, Still Illuminating the World

Lantern Walking Ahead

A collection of tribute poems for Jack Foley

Editor
Shajil Anthru

A Real Magazine Production

RM
REAL MAGAZINE PRODUCTIONS

For Jack Foley, Still Illuminating the World

Lantern Walking Ahead

A collection of tribute poems for Jack Foley

Editor: Shajil Anthru

Book production and design (c) 2024 by Real Magazine Productions

ISBN : 978-81-988393-5-0

Real Magazine Productions,
Trivandrum, Kerala, India.PIN 695011
Email:presidentrealmag@gmail.com
Website:https://realmagazinepro.com

ISBN: 978-81-988393-5-0

When the poet breathes his last,
those solitary lines
starts, to draw breath,
to live.

Some whisper like gentle strokes,
others swell into hurricanes
that tear the rooftops off the world
and rip the roofs from every belief.

Shajil Anthru

A Note by the Publisher

Jack Foley was born in August 1940 in Neptune, New Jersey. As an excellent student, and with the aid of his local library, Foley read widely and soon exploring the works of various poets. At fifteen he realized that, whatever else he was, he was now and forever a poet.

Foley's parents could not afford to send him to college, but he surprised them by winning scholarship money that enabled him to attend first Cornell University in Ithaca, New York, and then The University of California at Berkeley.

Foley worked hard as a graduate student at Berkeley and tried to keep his poetry going amid all the furor of "the sixties." Eventually, he dropped out of school. He wanted to become a poet. Foley also developed various techniques for writing and presenting poetry.

He persuaded his wife Adelle to help him perform what he called "choruses"--a word that conjured up both the ancient Greeks and the world of musical comedy. Foley created a "tap dance" poem which featured not only his words but a bit of the art his father taught him. Over the years, Foley published a multitude of books with various publishers—books of poetry, but books of essays as well.

Foley continues to write, perform, and think about poetry. 1955 to 2025 is a long journey in which Jack Foley had chosen poetry and writing for his "breathing". His presence in print and online media is commendable. He writes poetry, prose, essays, stories, dramas and had his signature in all genres of literature. Performance of Choruses and tap dance poems are innovative in the literature world.

During 1992-1995, he was awarded Poetry Grant from Oakland Arts Council .In 2010, he received a Lifetime Achievement Award from the Berkeley Poetry Festival, and June 5, 2010 was designated Jack Foley Day in Berkeley, California.

In 2018, he became the recipient of the Albert Nelson Marquis Lifetime Achievement Award.

In 2021, he became the first K M Anthru International Literature Award for his comprehensive contribution to literature from K M Anthru Foundation, India.

His poetry books often include accompanying CDs or cassette tapes on which Foley and Adelle perform his work. After Adelle's death in 2016, Foley has found a new love and performance partner in Sangye Land, daughter of poet Julie Rogers and stepdaughter of poet David Meltzer. Since 1988, he has hosted a show of interviews and poetry presentations on Berkeley radio station, KPFA.

In 2019, Monongahela Books released Foley's "Unmanageable Masterpiece", edited by Dana Gioia and Peter Whitfield. The book discusses and celebrates Foley's Visions & Affiliations:

His other creative works are:

- Telling It Slant (2024)
- Creative Death and Bridget and Andere Gedichte (poems selected and translated by Andreas Weiland) (2023)
- Collisions (2024)
- Ekphrazz (2024)
- The Light of Evening: A Brief Life of Jack Foley (2021)
- "A Backward Glance O'er Travel'd Roads," (2021)
- Author, 'When Sleep Comes: Shillelagh Songs' (2019)
- Author, 'The Dancer & the Dance: A Book of Distinctions' (2008-Present)
- Columnist, The Alsop Review (1998-Present)
- Co-Editor, Poetry Flash (1992-Present)
- Co-Performer, Poetry (1985-Present)
- Author, 'Grief Songs' (2016)
- Author, 'The Tiger and Other Tales' (2016)
- Author, 'RIVERRUN' (2016)
- Author, 'A California Beat Literary Timeline – The 1950s' (2014)
- Author, 'LIFE' (2014)
- Author, 'EYES: Selected Poems' (2013)
- Co-Author, 'Sketches Poetical' (2012)
- Author, 'Visions & Affiliations: A California Literary Timeline: Poets & Poetry 1940-2005,' Two Volumes (2011)
- Co-Author, 'Ahadada Reader 3' (2010)
- Author, 'Ash on an Old Man's Sleeve' (2009)
- Author, 'The Dancer and the Dance: A Book of Distinctions' (2008)
- Co-Author, 'Fennel in The Rain' (2007)
- Editor, 'ALL: A James Broughton Reader' (2006)
- Author, 'Greatest Hits 1974-2003' (2004)

- Editor, ‘Some Songs by Georges Brassens’ (2001)
- Editor, Contributor, ‘The Fallen Western Star Wars’ (2001)
- Author, ‘Foley’s Books: California Rebels, Beats and Radicals’ (2000)
- Author, ‘O Powerful Western Star’ (2000)
- Author, ‘Saint James’ (1998)
- Editor, ‘Advice to the Lovelorn’ (1998)
- Co-Editor, ‘New Poetry From California: Dead, Requiem’ (1998)
- Author, ‘Bridget’ (1997)
- Author, ‘Exiles’ (1996)
- Author, ‘O Her Blackness Sparkles! The Life and Times of the Batman Art Gallery, San Francisco, 1960-1965’ (1995)
- Author, ‘Inciting Big Joy’ (1993)
- Author, ‘Adrift’ (1993)
- Author, ‘Gershwin’ (1991)
- Author, ‘Letters/Lights-Words for Adelle’ (1987)
- Contributor, Bright Lights

Real Magazine Productions, the unique publishers from Kerala, India, presented his final book “Telling it Slant”, to the world in 2024. We were planning to have his another book published in 2025 when, Jack Foley left this world, early thhis November.

The readers will certainly find Jack Foley as the Synonym to Creativity and also as the Unquestioning master at Poetry.Through this book “ Lantern Walking Ahead”, his friends and fellow poets pay tribute to Late Jack Foley.

✷ ✷ ✷

Lantern Walking Ahead

CONTENTS

The Silent Bond

Shajil Anthru

Shajil Anthru

Born in Trivandrum, Kerala ,India on 27 January 1968 is a multilingual , multigenre writer who published more than 15 books. He is Chief Editor of Litterateur Redefining World, a transnational magazine instituted in August 2020. K M Anthru Foundation is established by Shajil Anthru in memory of his father K M Anthru, also a writer in Malayalam who passed away on December 2020. K M Anthru International Prize wasA instituted by him which is presented to selected writers and artists globally. Jack Foley was the first recipient of K M Anthru International Prize for Literature in 2021 for his comprehensive contribution to literature.

Shajil Anthru is also the Founder of Zeroism - a philosophy which defines the current era. He also possess the Fishbone poetry founder, a new poetic style in literature. Also he surpassed Ernest Hemingway's six word short story in three and one word short stories.

On August 2020, Shajil Anthru met Jack Foley through an email, the relation which transcending beyond a friend to "undefined" relation. Almost everyday , both found time to interact which strenghten their bond day by day. Jack Foley became a family member of Shajil Anthru.

“The Silent Bond” is the first chapter of Shajil Anthru’s new book “Verses We Never Finished: A Friendship in Poetry and Grief” which is a critical analyis of Jack Foley’s works .

Who was Shajil Anthru for Jack Foley?

Foreword written for the book “Redefining Literature: New Order of the Day” ; Author :Shajil Anthru: ISBN :979-8708423153

From time to time we need to be reminded that the poet's adventures in the labyrinthine fields of language represent something that is good for you. Not merely entertaining or interesting or even imaginative but good for you: even healing. Shelley famously asserted in his "Defence of Poetry" that poets were "the unacknowledged legislators of the world." More recently, Yuval Noah Harari asserted in his book, Sapiens that the human imagination was an immensely important factor in our evolutionary development. In "An Apology for Poetry," the great English poet Sir Philip Sidney saw the poet as the mediator between worlds--the transcendent and the historical. Nature's world, says Sidney, "is brazen, the poets only deliver a golden"--which is to say, among other things, that only poets deliver the possibility of radical change. Not for nothing did Plato fear the presence of poets in his authoritative Republic! Now, here is Shajil Anthru saying the same thing as all these others but saying it now, in an era of inhumane authoritarians and pandemics. We need his words badly. He is telling us something we know but need to know with passion.

Response writtend for the book, "UNVEILING THE NEW WORLD" , Author :Shajil Anthru ;ISBN-13 : 979-8890663887

SHAJIL ANTHRU, UNVEILING THE NEW WORLD

SHAJIL ANTHRU'S EFFORT

> Du mußt dein Leben ändern.
> ("You must change your life.")
> —Rilke

There are times in every writer's life when it becomes necessary to take stock, to sum up what one has accomplished or failed to accomplish. Unveiling the New World gives us access to such a moment in the writing life of the poet, essayist, publisher, engineer Shajil Anthru, whose fundamental mission—his life's work—is nothing less than to redefine the world. In this he is in the great tradition of Rilke and Shelley—even of Whitman. The "unveiling" we see so eloquently described in this book is an indication of where this immensely complex, immensely valuable project is coming along.

It is also necessarily an introduction to the work—to the mind—of Shajil Anthru. Though the author's mind is complex indeed, you will find that the work here is deliberately articulated with the utmost clarity. The book offers the reader not the struggle with the angel but the delight of good fellowship, wit, and imagination. The photograph of the author's marvelous daughter, Roshni, smiling broadly and crying out, "Hai!" would be worth the price of admission.

"If I am asked to name my role model," writes Anthru, "I would certainly say it is Leonardo da Vinci. He taught me that only an engineer can be an excellent teacher and artist/poet. Also, only an artist/poet can be an excellent engineer. He taught me not to be confined in a single discipline. This reflects in my writing and application of engineering knowledge."

The American critic Paul de Man wittily labelled his essay on Jean-Jacques Rousseau, author of the Confessions, "excuses." You will find no such necessity here. Shajil Anthru is a serious thinker who inhabits a serious planet which he sincerely wishes to change—for the better. This book is a hymn to the radical openness of his mind.

The Silent Bond

On August 13, 2020, I received an email from dddmonster1940. It is none other than Jack Foley. He wrote:

"Dear Editor,
Shajil Anthru asked me to send a submission for the September issue.
To give you some choice, I've attached four poems and a story. I hope you'll find something here that you like.
Here is a short bio:
Jack Foley has published 17 books of poetry, 5 books of criticism, a book of stories, and a 1300-page "chronoencyclopedia," Visions & Affiliations: California Poetry 1940-2005. He became well known through his multi-voiced performances with his late wife, Adelle, also a poet. He currently performs with his new life partner, Sangye Land. He has presented poetry on radio station KPFA since 1988 and has received two Lifetime Achievement Awards. A new book of Foley's poetry, When Sleep Comes: Shillelagh Songs has recently appeared, and Duet of Polygon, a collaboration with Japanese poet Maki Starfield, is forthcoming. Poet/scholars Dana Gioia and Peter Whitfield have edited Jack Foley's Unmanageable Masterpiece, a book of essays dealing with Foley's Visions & Affiliations."

Of course, the email had attachment which included four poems and one short story. All poems are versatile, powerful to penetrate your heart. The composition of each poem differed, which shows his exceptional intellectual and creative power. I was fortunate to read his poetry "LOVE" - the first piece of Jack Foley in my life.

LOVE
is a two-sided mirror
my love is reflected in one side
your love is reflected in the other
but it is one mirror
and it turns

I was mesmerized by the compactness, yet, unbounded meaning and impact of this short poem. Normally, a mirror reflects only one face: the reflection of the viewer. How beautifully Jack Foley challenges this by calling love a two-sided mirror. Love is a shared value that must reflect two people at once. When the poet says when "my love is reflected in one side / your love is reflected in the other", the "I love you, you love me" is reminded in reader's heart. In this poem, each partner sees not their own face but they feel the love, the other directs toward them.

The significant emphasize is on the duality (two sides, two loves), even though the object is singular. The lovers are not looking into separate mirrors; they are looking at opposite faces of the same piece of glass. This diminishes the distance between "mine" and "yours." The reflection each sees is generated by the same source. When the poet says "and it turns", one can recreate the turning mirror catching light from every degree of rotation. Foley says that when the mirror spins, the image of my love and the image of your love are no longer confined to opposite sides. At certain angles of turn, the two reflections coincide perfectly, becoming unidentifiable or ONE. Who can give a better definition for LOVE than Jack Foley? The mirror does not belong to either lover; the lovers belong to the mirror. The true love abolishes the boundary between self and other by making each partner's devotion the very surface on which the other's devotion appears.

In return, I wrote:

a silvered wafer suspended between two hearts.
a moonlit orchid, trembling, open.
a dawn-lit rose, dew-kissed, burning.
holding both our fires
without scorching, either.
like a planet remembering its twin star,
it revolves.
Petals of my orchid slide across your rose,
scarlet bleeding into indigo,
indigo bleeding back.
For one trembling instant
the two flowers occupy the same space—
a single, impossible bloom
that is neither mine nor yours
but a hush where names dissolve.

Jack Foley's other poems were
"IN THE BEGINNING WAS THE WORST
AND THE WORST WAS WITH GOD
—Irish proverb
CALIFORNIA and
SHIP OF FOOLS.

The only short story he sent was "MAN ON WHOM THE SUN HAS GONE DOWN" and was published in the September edition 2020.

"Man on Whom the Sun Has Gone Down" is a reflective short story that evokes the delicateness of human identity. The story follows a first-person narrative and the reader see a writer who finds solace in dreams, illusions, and fictional companions—both human and animal—only to justify the raw cruelty within himself when a rat invades his home.

The story opens with chilling daytime fears:

"There is more terror in the day than in the night. Only today I saw a man berate his child and strike him. I might have been the child. I saw an automobile swerving around a corner, going too fast. I might have been a pedestrian struck down by the automobile. Indeed, I might have been one of the leaves that fell from the tree this morning. I read on the internet that someone in my neighborhood had been mugged. I walk alone, great distances, with no protection. I too might be mugged."

These threats are universal. Yet the narrator lives them through deep empathy. His heart sobers at others' anguish, extending even to nature.

"Indeed, I might have been one of the leaves that fell from the tree this morning."

This reflection reveals a true litterateur, one who erases boundaries between self and world.

By contrast, night offers release:

"During the night, I can close my eyes and enter the dark world. During the night, I can dream or enter a void in which I no longer need to cling to my identity. My age no longer matters. My name no longer matters. Sometimes dead people visit me, but they carry no fear with them. I feel it is only concern for the living."

A man with open eyes and a man with closed eyes presents opposite poles. As a writer, the narrator is adapted to the companionship of the nonexistent:

"I am a writer, so I am used to the companionship of people who do not exist. They flit inside me constantly. Men, women, children. I have friends among the beasts as well. Dogs and cats but also deer, birds, wolves, coyotes, even the fierce tiger, the bear and the fierce lion... They hold no terror for me. I know they are illusions, creatures that tell me of myself. You may call them metaphors if you like, but for me, they are beast friends."

Only a master writer could introduce a character so skillfully, zeroing the line between human and creature. The narrator asserts,

"I am usually a very gentle man. The presence of violence of any kind upsets me deeply. I didn't believe I had it in me to kill."

This revelation evokes suspense. Has this gentle soul become a murderer? The readers cannot resist their anxiety. The greatest strengths of the story are the psychological depth and the poetic brilliance.

The bold rat becomes a mirror. The act of killing is not triumphant but shocking. This swivel from compassion to finality is devastatingly human, reminding us the Dostoevsky's underground man or Camus's stranger in its unwavering self-accusation.

Not a single word could be edited; the language is perfectly poetic, transporting us into a world of thoughts, dreams, and the fragile surroundings we dwell.

The title itself is a masterstroke.

The title "Man on Whom the Sun Has Gone Down" is a direct reference to Ezra Pound's early poem "The Tree" (from his 1909 collection Personae), where Pound writes;

"I stood still and was a tree amid the wood,
Knowing the truth of things unseen before;
Of Daphne and the laurel bough
And that god-feasting couple old
That grew elm-oak amid the wold.
'Twas not until the gods had been
Kind unto me, that I saw
The man on whom the sun has gone down."

"The man on whom the sun has gone down" in Pound's poem, shows us a person undergoing a transformation. As if, a man, banished from ordinary life, giving vision of hidden truths.

But in Foley's short story, this line reflects the philosophy - what begins as a potential transcendence ends in guilt and self-loathing. By killing the rat, his "brother," the narrator extinguishes something vital in himself. The sun no longer shines on him. He has become cursed and spiritually dead.

Ultimately, "Man on Whom the Sun Has Gone Down" is a small masterpiece of quiet horror. The true monster is not the rat but the man, and the real nightmares live in broad daylight. The title lingers like an eternal accusation, reminding us that the sun sets not only on the day but on the soul that betrays its own gentleness.

K M ANTHRU INTERNATIONAL PRIZE FOR HIS COMPREHENSIVE CONTRIBUTION IN LITERATURE 2021

* * *

Atque Vale

Christopher Bernard

" I wrote it the morning after the late night posting on Facebook where I first learned of Jack's passing."

Christopher Bernard is an award-winning poet, novelist and playwright; he is also co-editor and founder of the webzine Caveat Lector. His novels include A Spy in the Ruins ("one of the best American novels since Thomas Pynchon and William Gass," Miguel de Cervantes–award winning novelist Juan Goytisolo), Voyage to a Phantom City ("an enormous achievement," award-winning translator Peter Bush), and Meditations on Love and Catastrophe at The Liars' Cafe ("puts one in mind of Ulysses as much as Naked Lunch," award-winning poet Ernest Hilbert). His third collection of poems, The Socialist's Garden of Verses, won a PEN Oakland Josephine Miles Award and was named one of the "Top 100 Indie Books of 2021" by Kirkus Reviews. His most recent books are the middle-grade children's stories, the first in the "Otherwise" series, If You Ride A Crooked Trolley . . . and The Judgment Of Biestia, which won an Independent Press Award in Preteen Fiction in 2025. His most recent play is Ubu Triumphant! A Farce in Five Fits, an adaptation and updating of Alfred Jarry's Ubu Roi for the age of Donald Trump. In 2019, he received an Albert Nelson Marquis Lifetime Achievement Award.

Atque Vale

Hail, Giacomo, poet who thrust
enigmas of language to the edge of paradox,
invented a genre or two, exploded
myths of meaning and freed the poem
from hobbles of cliché and the received folly
of academia and publishers afraid
of readers as much as their own shadows;
whose warm heart comforted the peculiar loneliness
of poetry, and spread the word on the word
from page to podium to KPFA.
Hail, Giacomo, loyal champion and friend,
though we tangled over much, we agreed on this:
the love of good friends and the love of the word
are among the strongest shelters and shields
against the raging storm of the world.
Hail, noble mind, powerful spirit and heart,
marvelous poet, munificent lover of art,
one of the few known to me who deserve the grand title
of "genius," rarest of flowers in the human fields,
where blossoms have been many but fruits few where they fell.
Hail, Giacomo, hail and farewell.

For Jack Foley

✷ ✷ ✷

Yumiko Tsumura

Yumiko Tsumura is a poet and translator of modern Japanese poetry. After receiving BA and MA, and PhD residency in American literature at Kansei Gakuin University in Japan, she joined International Writing Program(IWP) and earned MFA in poetry and translation from the University of Iowa.

New Directions published her books of translation in collaboration with Samuel Grolmes: Kazuko Shiraishi's selected poems *Let Those Who Appear* (2002), *My Floating Mother, City* (2009), Ryuichi Tamura's poem "*The World Without Words*" in New Directions 22, and Yumiko Kurahashi's 3 short stories in New Directions 24, 26, 29. Also cccbooks published *Tamura Ryuichi Poems 1946 - 1998, 2000.* New Directions published her translation of Kazuko Shiraishi's selected poems *Sea, Land, Shadow* (2017).

Her books of own poetry include *Woman of March*, Finishing Line Press, 2017, *Man of Peace*, Black Mountain Press, 2020, *All in One*, Black Mountain Press, 2021. She continues to publish her poems in major American Poetry Journals. She published "*The days with Kakuko Shiraishi, friendship* - as her translator" In *Modern Poetry Journal memorial issue for Kazuko Shiraishi*, October, 2024. and Carillon Street, December, 2025.

Recently she has donated the works of three masters of modern Japanese literature---Ryuichi Tamura, Yumiko Kurahashi and Kazuko Shiraishi: original signed books, manuscripts, correspondences as well as her books of translation of their works to Stanford University East Asian Library, and to IWP, the University of Iowa for permanent preservation.

Yumiko Tsumura

Your Gift

- to Jack Foley in praise of your eyes

You wrote a Jacket blurb for my poetry book Woman of March.

"These delicate poems are alive with deep silence in which they occur.
They are not haiku but haiku-like, suddenly emerging as epiphanies—enigma —upon the white paper.
They are a testimony to a life lived not in the light of intellect but in specific, deep consciousness.
To encounter YumikoTsumura's poems is to encounter
something deep, elliptical, passionate: "spots of time."

Your poetry activities exude compassion.

August 9, 2025 is your 85th Birthday,
and it is the day of the Atomic Bombing of Nagasaki, 1945

Now, allow me to give you
The final line of "Reunion" by the greatest post war poet, Ryuichi Tamura,
"You   the earth is rough"
Positive warning to us in incessant wars across the globe.

Coping with dark humanity surrounding us,
You are a rainbow
In the twilight of my life.

Jack loved many of my poems

Jack loved many of my poems. From "Woman of Straw" he said "Days went by her like paper." Not like leaves: like paper.
Also, he loved lines "I wash my eyes/ in the May light": " What I want to be / is raining softly."

From "Care Partner"...

My tongue dove deep
Into my roots in the village
I devoured the memories of
the sea and the soil

Even with broken wings, we will
soar again
together

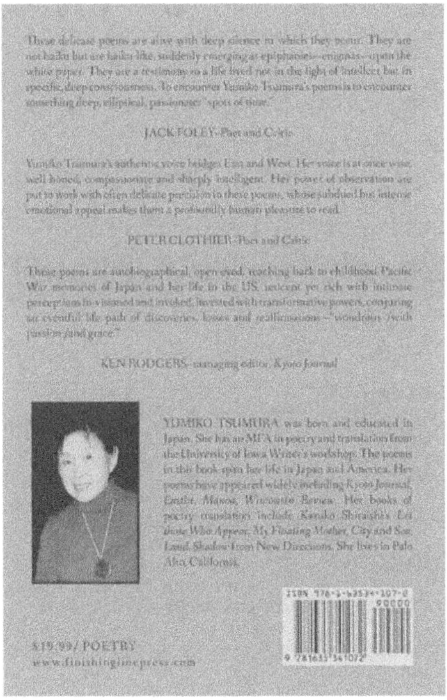

These delicate poems are alive with deep silence to which they point. They are not haiku but are haiku-like, suddenly emerging as epiphanies—enigmas—upon the white paper. They are a testimony to a life lived not in the light of intellect but in specific, deep consciousness. To encounter Yumiko Tsumura's poems is to encounter something deep, elliptical, passionate: "spots of time."

JACK FOLEY–Poet and Critic

Yumiko Tsumura's authentic voice bridges East and West. Her voice is at once wise, well honed, compassionate and sharply intelligent. Her powers of observation are put to work with often delicate precision in these poems, whose subdued but intense emotional appeal makes them a profoundly human pleasure to read.

PETER CLOTHIER–Poet and Critic

These poems are autobiographical, open-eyed, reaching back to childhood Pacific War memories of Japan and her life in the US, reticent yet rich with intimate perceptions envisioned and invoked, invested with transformative powers, conjuring an eventful life path of discoveries, losses and reaffirmations—"wondrous /with passion /and grace."

KEN RODGERS–managing editor, *Kyoto Journal*

YUMIKO TSUMURA was born and educated in Japan. She has an MFA in poetry and translation from the University of Iowa Writer's workshop. The poems in this book span her life in Japan and America. Her poems have appeared widely including *Kyoto Journal, Exile, Manoa, Wisconsin Review*. Her books of poetry translation include Kazuko Shiraishi's *Let those Who Appear, My Floating Mother, City and Sea, Land, Shadow* from New Directions. She lives in Palo Alto, California.

ISBN 978-1-63534-107-2

$19.99/ POETRY
www.finishinglinepress.com

✳ ✳ ✳

JACK!

Andreas Weiland

Jack -
You spoke of Adelle, your wife
You did not forget her
You spoke of friends who went
But I know, friendship mattered
You spoke of the ordinary things of life
LOVE DEATH
FEARS and HOPES
Sexuality
Poetry
Yes, the films!
How long ago that you saw them!
The Maltese Falcon
The Lost Weekend
Kiss Me, Deadly
The atomic bomb, in a box
You sat in the darkness
Seeing them again
Holding hands with Sanye, your friend
The darkness envelops you now

It is no longer the darkness of living rooms
The night lights went out
For you went
Like others before you
And it is you now
who is remembered
I think of the photo you sent
And I think, Was it in premonition?
Forebodings, suddenly
Strange moment
Mere chance?
You said, I don´t recognize me any more
And I wrote you,
It´s like a return
It is you, your roots, Jack
You look like an old Irish bard
And fishermen
In their boats, off the coast -
Was it, off Aran?
And Flaherty came to mind
Another return to the movies...
I thought of a poet, to boot
A man you cared for:
Yeats
We all remember you -
like this, Jack
And though your body changed
and the features of the face are no longer the same
that you saw in your youth
you saw yourself in that picture

The face of a poet who remains
although it is no longer tangible, now, the flesh
The voice remains
The voice of a poet
Yes, I hear it still
It resonates
in me

Enger, Germany, in November, 2025

* * *

Rafael Jesús González

Rafael Jesús González, Prof. Emeritus of Creative Writing & Literature and Mexican & Latin American Studies, four times nominated for a Pushcart Prize, honored by the National Council of Teachers of English for his writing 2003, received a César E. Chávez Lifetime Award 2013, and one by the city of Berkeley 2015; named Berkeley's first Poet Laureate 2017. Also a visual artist, he has exhibited at the Oakland Museum of California, the Mexican Museum of San Francisco, and other venues. http://rjgonzalez.blogspot.com/

Here are the attached are two of Rafael Jesus Gonzalez poems that Jack particularly liked:
"Lección/Lesson" and
"Luna Sobre Gaza/Moon Over Gaza".

Luna sobre Gaza

La luna sobre Gaza,
su luz sanadora
velada por el humo,
es como luna de sangre
teñida por la sangre
del niño muerto
en los brazos de su madre,
la madre muriendo
al llanto de su niña,
el padre muerto
en montón de escombros,
los sufriendo y muriendo
de heridas y de hambre.
En guerra son siempre
los inocentes que más pagan
— ¿jamás aprenderemos,
oh hijos de Abraham?
Madrina luna sigue mirando
de río a mar.

Moon Over Gaza

The moon over Gaza,
her healing light
veiled by the smoke,
is like a blood moon
stained with the blood
of the innocent—
the child dead
in his mother's arms,
the mother dying
to her daughter's wails,
the father dead
in a pile of rubble,
the suffering and dying
of wounds and of hunger.
In war it is always
the innocent who pay most
— will we never learn,
oh children of Abraham?
Godmother moon looks on
from river to sea.

Lección

a Julín y Maripep

Después de cuarenta y pico de años
volví a ver a mis amigos
de América del Sur.
Nos habíamos conocido,
    de jovencitos,
en Atenas, cuna, nos dicen,
de la democracia, tal como fue.
Luego nos volvimos a encontrar
en Madrid de la España fascista.
    Éramos jóvenes,
nos mofábamos
    de los monumentos tiesos,
de las palabras constipadas
de un tal Calvo Sotelo.
        Nos reíamos mucho.

Ahora me enseñan su Montevideo,
    sus monumentos,
uno de ellos a los desaparecidos,
grandes paredes de vidrio
grabado con un montón de nombres.
Me cuentan como había sido
    su propia dictadura:
el temor constante;
el amigo, el pariente, el vecino
    desaparecido;
el no poder hablar abiertamente
ni con el más íntimo amigo,

el hermano;
como no atreverse decirle al hijo, hija
cuando venían a casa
con ideas repugnantes
que se les habían enseñado en la escuela,
— "No es así." —
por temor de que lo repitieran en el aula;
el constante temor del toque en la puerta;
la tortura, la muerte, el desaparecer.

Ahora en mi país cuando hablo
en oposición al gobierno,
nuestro propio fascismo,
hay bobos que me dicen
—"Si estuvieras allá" —
(refiriéndose al país
que al momento
se antoja el enemigo)
— "no podrías decirlo." —
(significando — "¡Cállate!
¡Cierra la boca!")

Idiotas — si una libertad
se guarda encerrada
como una guitarra sin cuerdas,
no es libertad
y pronto nos llegará
el toque en la puerta,
pronto desapareceremos.

Lesson

to Julín & Maripep

After forty some years
I again saw my friends
of South America.
We had known each other,
from youth,
in Athens, cradle they tell us,
of democracy such as it was.
Then we met again
in Madrid of the fascist Spain.
We were young,
we ridiculed
the stiff monuments,
the constipated words
of a certain Calvo Sotelo.
We laughed a lot.

Now they show me their Montevideo,
their monuments,
one of them to the disappeared,
big walls of glass
engraved with a pile of names.
They tell me how it had been,
their own dictatorships:
the constant fear;
the friend, the relative, the neighbor
disappeared;
their not being able to speak openly
not even with the most intimate friend,
one's brother;
how not dare to tell the son, the daughter
when they came home
with repugnant ideas

they had learned at school,
— "It is not so." —
for fear they would repeat it in the classroom;
the constant fear of the knock on the door;
the torture, death, disappearance.

Now in my country when I speak
in opposition to the government,
our very own fascism,
there are fools who tell me
— "If you were over there" —
(referring to the country
which at the moment
we imagine our enemy)
— "you would not be able to say it." —
(meaning — "Be quiet!
Shut your mouth up!")

Idiots — if a freedom
is kept locked
like a guitar without strings,
it is not freedom
and soon shall come to us
the knock on the door,
soon we will disappear.

* * *

Xanthi Hondrou-Hill

Xanthi Hondrou-Hill is an award winning poetess from Greece. She holds a Masters Degree in German Literature and Linguistics, and postmasters degrees in Journalism and Public Relations Management. She worked among others at the University of Stuttgart as lecturer and the General Consulate of Greece in Stuttgart as Public Relations Consultant, creating the DAYS OF GREEK CULTURE. She got an honorary doctorate from CIESART in Spain and is the chairperson of the Linguistic Rights and Translations Committee of PEN Greece. She is the founder and director of the International Poetry Festival of Naoussa, in Greece.

POETIC HABITAT

The poets live
in their poems.
They are born in them
they grow up there
they are raised by the words
in the spaces they breath
they are resting on the punctuation
and even when they leave
they exist in the white of every piece of
paper
at the edge of every pencil
and in the infinite possibilities of
expression in every language of the world...

✷ ✷ ✷

debora Ewing

“Jack was a force, as I've heard many others say, and he impacted me in a way that I resisted at first.

I was tasked with laying out his Magnum Opus, *Creative Death*, for Igneus Press. His direction ran counter to everything I knew about poetry books and layout design, so of course I am forever changed for the better.

Jack and I often "traded licks" - I would respond to his poems with some of my own. I had a recent email glitch that lost some of my original words to him, but the attached is exemplary of our communications.

Jack was fond of "pairings" - two poems whose voices interplayed like jazz musicians. My poem 'refrain/credits' is published in my book *chorus echo*, released by Igneus Press this year. I don't know whether Jack had published 'Telling It Slant/Post Xmas'”

debora Ewing

Telling It Slant/Post Xmas

An old man looks
At one of his books.
When I become one
With the Rock of Ages,
What will be left
Except these pages.
Down the tunnel of time
Goes my labored rhyme.
Whatever the quest,
I did my best.
In times remote
Perhaps some scribe'll
Ignore the Bible
And cite a quote.
Though it may be cant,
I told it slant.

- Jack Foley

refrain / credits

this book is to remember
those days of tea & freer words
with a man of my own making

we've gone too far into that desert
where everything's a bone
and meat is precious

your soul becomes more
opaque with every liner note
a choice of font is permanent

but once upon a time
fox pups played in the snow
like old black & white movies

- debora Ewing

✷ ✷ ✷

Jovelyn D. Richard

The Space Around Jack Foley

- to Jack Foley in praise of your eyes

A conversation with Jack
On KPFA's : Jovelyn and Jack
Was to enter an alternative universe
A place of questions
Memories
And humor
That doubled as a doorway, ajar
Not just a broadcast
A deep listening.
A language ceremony
Where the "I" dissolved
Into conscious conversation
Or, as Jack would reply, something like...
"Maybe we're unconscious
Where the real stories exist."
Jack believed in the collective breath.
"Poetry isn't mine, it's ours.
It's what the air knows before we do."
Breathe
Compliments of his brilliance

He shook off
Like the friendly Labrador in the rain
But the compliments and the rain continued.
Not because he doubted them
But because he knew
Brilliance was a shared inheritance
"If I'm brilliant," he grinned,
"Then so are the shadows that shaped me."
Jack taught me
That the space around a word
Is as sacred
As the word itself.
Jack.
I'm sitting in the space now,
Now that Jack is gone.
Waiting for a word
To describe his absence
a space around a word
Jack

✳ ✳ ✳

Jovelyn Richards is an international American writer, director, and performance artist based in Honolulu, Hawai'i. Her work explores ancestral memory, nonlinear time, and ceremonial storytelling as tools for healing and social critique. She is the author of Songs of Water: A Southern Novel of Mosaic Myths and Memories, and creator of Working Hobo-Clown, a solo performance blending satire and archetypal inquiry. Jovelyn's performances have appeared at The Marsh SF, National Black Theatre Festival, Los Angeles Women's Theatre Festival, and NOLA Fringe. She holds an MA and MFA in Humanities and Creative Inquiry, and mentors MFA students at the California Institute of Integral Studies, where she also serves as an independent contractor. She is an affiliate of the Playwrights' Center in Minneapolis and artistic director of Writefully Yours Performance Academy (WYPA). Her work invites audiences into transformative spaces where myth, memory, and social commentary converge.

Emilija Todorova

Emilija Todorova is a Macedonian Australian author. Born is Skopje, Macedonia, she has been living in Australia since 1989. She is a recipient of numerous awards for her poetry and prose in former Yugoslavia, Macedonia, Australia, USA and Italy. Her poetry book "Gravity" won the "Stoyan Hristov" award for best poetry work by an expat at the prestigious international poetry festival Struga Poetry Evenings in 2022. Emilija's poems have been included in over fifteen anthologies and poetry selections and published in various international literary magazines.

JACK FOLEY IS HERE

Don’t believe those
who say he’s gone
he’s just taken absence without leave
(he never sought permission to live either)
with no intention to desert
the word and the world

not an abandonment –
absence is the root
of possibilities

can't you see him
here he is
shaping syllables into voices:

I wish to know*	Can you whisper**
what I have done	that you have done
in this life only	something in the world

their echo climbs
the tower of conscience
he built out of mirrors
we are too afraid to look in

* From the poem “How Am I How Am I” by Jack Foley 2025
** From the poem “ Selfie” by Jack Foley 2025

✷ ✷ ✷

Elizabeth Nisperos

MVP – Jack Foley, Most Valuable Poet

artist & calligrapher friend of Jack, also her teacher and mentor.

Which sort of Jack is Jack Foley?

Jack Frost? Authentic Foley warm,friendly,inclusive,smiling

Jack and the Beanstalk? A giant writing in the clouds of Poetry

Jack Daniels? Whiskey, intoxicated with enchantment enigma

Jack and Jill? Jack and Adele and Sangye, lover in love always

Jack the Ripper? He ripped poetry out of his entire molecular soul, ripping out words to console holes to create whole

Jack in the Box? He was in and out of the box creating poems of infinitesimal but stellar echoes in the galaxy.

Jack be Nimble, Jack be Quick? Agile, Flexible with whimsical poems, scarcastic to evil policies, activist ready to defend democracy pointing out injustice.

Jack O'Lantern? Witty outwitting devils oppressing freedom of choices, expression, a guiding light inside the pumpkin of darkness.

Jack mentor and friend sends out his written words via email stirring the laughter, tears, silence inside the human heart.

The MVP of Poetry, vibrating at KPFA radio every Tuesday to stir love of poetry whoever wants to listen,to awaken, to enlighten.

✳ ✳ ✳

Elizabeth Nisperos toggles between the arts and sciences. She is a former Commissioner in South San Francisco Cultural Arts Commission, Council Member of SF Calligraphy Guild. She is an award winning artist/calligrapher in painting, calligraphy. She demoed in international calligraphy event, solo exhibition in San Francisco International Center and San Mateo County Fairs, featured in a gallery and books, composed religious song featured in Rome and composed song for her city. She's a regular writing contributor in ESC and Patch online news magazines, Alphabet calligraphy journal and submitted poems in journals Fresh Bread, and Editor for Blue and Gold Church Archconfraternity. She received outstanding community award for creating a computer literacy program for unemployed folks at Daly City. With background in Sciences and to earn money to support being an artist, she taught Biology and Chemistry, later worked in Network Operations, Computer Programming, Software Engineering & Robotics. She is a STEAM(Science, Technology, Engineering, Arts and Mathematics) mentor for children, regularly attends STEAM international summit events. She is also award winning techie having received award certificates from Google Code Corp, Computer World Honours Laureate Medal, project member, Outstanding Effort and Dedication for IBM project. Her technical paper also won first prize in scanning and imaging international events.

Anthony Holdsworth

Jack's genius merits a tribute volume. Anthony Holdsworth has a considerable reputation as a painter and none as a poet, though he has written poetry all his life. He read the poems included here on Cover to Cover when Jack interviewed him

Anthony Holdsworth dedicated the poem Nicaragua '84 to Nina Serrano, who shared cover to Cover with Jack for some years, because she and Anthony Holdsworth were involved in the solidarity movement around the Sandinista revolution.

"The Road Home" accompanied his painting "The Way Home" (reproduced here below the poem) in his catalogue "Cities on the Water" published for his exhibition in 2008 at the Newmark gallery in San Francisco.

NICARAGUA 1984

For Nina Serrano

Where tyrants could not quiet
the people's heart
and parrots gather
In the golden shade,

In a dusty land
where hope beats like a drum,
In paradise at war
where children's laughter
sparkles in the sun

The people sing of liberty
in tongues of flame
and love awakens
simple as the earth,
the sun, the rain

Sept 1984

THE ROAD HOME

There was a time when watery highways led
'Sul nave per mare partiró'
out magic casements opening on the foam
cross waters bluer than the bluest eye,
darker than wine.

There is a time of rage on pavements,
shattered asphalt, shards of glass.
A labyrinthine grid where
limos dark as petroleum
glide past the captive streets.

Heap of abandoned blanket on
hard, cold ground
moves, coughs, groans.
We let it languish
prostrate and vanquished
on our road home

2003

MY EXPERIENCE OF JACK FOLEY

I first heard Jack's sonorous voice on Cover to Cover on KPFA in the late 90s. I knew people at the station so it wasn't long before we met. I was immediately enamored of his erudite intellect and his warm, avuncular nature. I was also stuck by the immediacy and accessibility of his poetry.

Despite my British origins, we bonded over his Irish, Italian extraction because I have a passion for Irish literature and have lived in Italy. We both shared a respect for tradition as well as an iconoclastic dislike of the Academy. Though Jack clearly possessed the skill and knowledge of an academician.

I was delighted when Jack chose my Oakland paintings as cover art for Oh Powerful Western Star and Foley's Books.

I painted two portraits of him while we sat at an outdoor table at Caffè 817 in Old Oakland. During our meandering conversation, he demonstrated his uncanny insight. He observed that although I identified closely with my subjects on the street, I, like most artists, operated from the viewpoint of an outsider. He also declared that he could see the influence of my interest in astrology in my paintings. When he finished posing, I gave him his favorite portrait.

For his part, Jack interviewed me twice on his program, once about my poetry and once to discuss an English/ Italian bilingual book I had published on the experience of painting in Italy.

I happened to phone him the week before he died. For some years we had been communicating by phone or email. He told me that he was concentrating on organizing his life's work. "I'm 85, and I've observed that not many people live much longer." We joked about the burdens of age and decided that it was high time we got together face to face. We agreed to meet for lunch the following week. The next Monday I was shocked to receive news of his departure from this realm.

Every moment I spent with Jack, whether alone or together with our families, was a pleasure. His generosity, his humor, his radiant personality will linger in my memory.

* * *

Anthony Holdsworth was born in England in 1945. He was introduced to oil painting in high school by the New England painter, Loring Coleman. Holdsworth embarked on a painting career while working as Head of Outdoor Restoration for the Uffizi Gallery in Florence, Italy after the flood of 1966. He continued his studies at the Bournemouth College of Art in England where he studied with master draftsman Samuel Rabin and color theorist Jon Fish and at the San Francisco Art Institute where he studied with Julius Hatofsky, Bruce McGaw and Fred Martin. He has shown with major galleries in Oakland, San Francisco, Sacramento and Los Angeles. He has participated in two exhibitions at the Oakland Museum. He was included in the California Cityscapes exhibition at the San Diego Museum. Most recently his work was selected for the 'de Young Open 2020' at the de Young Museum in San Francisco. He was a recipient of WESTAF-NEA fellowship in 1990. His work is in corporate and private collections worldwide. Website: www.anthonyholdsworth.com

Nina Serrano

A Jack Foley related commentary

Without ever a lunch or dinner date or couples date
we were friends because our work in poetry and radio was joint
but mostly conducted online once that came into use.

I kept track of your changing partners and
always sent regards to them.
I did not realize until the devastating news of your passing
how much a vital support you were to me.

I am floating around unanswered without you.

I write a new poem but it doesn't matter as much because you are not reading.
It.

✷ ✷ ✷

Dale Jensen

I've known Jack since 1985, when I met him at an early reading of his at Larry Blake's. He was proud of being a contrarian, but he was a beautiful and compassionate human being, too, a magnificent poet, a cultural historian (in poetry, film, the popular music of the early Twentieth Century, and much more), and a friend, inspiration, and guide to the real world for so many of us. He defined his own space by being himself, and we can all remember the wonder of him and grow from it.

I really miss him, as do a lot of other people. Besides his brilliance as a poet and critic, he was brilliant as a human being. We'll all miss him, but he'll (I hope) always be among us.

Dale Jensen

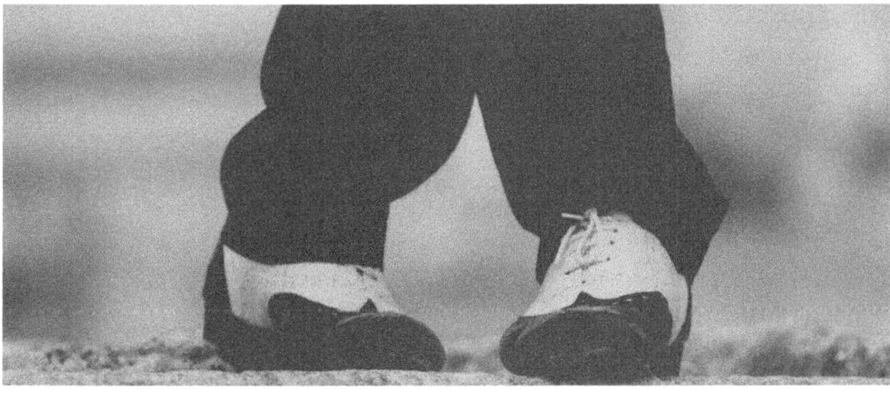

Tapdance (for Jack Foley)

the sky is writing itself over in black
deceased souls are turning into clouds
you might say
but that's what you would say
if one of your best friends had died yesterday

up there where you can't see there's only mist
about a century ago his father inhabited vaudeville
palled around with george m cohan
clouds like that are far enough away from the world now
that you could call them mythical landscapes
or memory too insubstantial for words

but your art of this century is poetry
something you'd hear like a tapdance
and oh maybe he'd tell a few stories
someone who's always been of the ages tells stories
stories and poems set higher than any specific past or future
any high chorus kicks any kicks at all
and you might score his heroic syllables as symphony
or dance or the approving ravings of baudelaire
whose mortal moves are up there too somewhere
the earth still vibrates with both of them
they too still part of the big dance

***

Dale Jensen was born in Oakland, California, and has degrees in psychology from UC Berkeley and the University of Toronto. He has seven books and six chapbooks of poetry out, has co-coordinated several poetry reading series in the Bay Area, and edited the poetry magazine Malthus in the 1980's.

Hadaa Sendoo

The Golden Autumn Is Infinitely Beautiful

for Jack

A silent leaf
Left the tree
And slowly waved its hand

That's the poet Jack, a friend I've never met
It seemed as if I saw him strolling in the morning breeze
And following Yeats

* * *

Hadaa Sendoo is a prize-winning Mongolian poet. His poems have been translated into more than 40 languages and he has published more than 20 books of poetry, Recent titles include: I don't need a funeral (Arabic 2020), Song of Nomadic Moonlight (Bengali, 2021), Der Wind (2022, in German), The Love that Came to Me (2023, in Mongolian). He has received the Poet of the Millennium Award (India 2000); The Mongolian Writers' Union Prize (Mongolia 2009); The Pinnacle of Achievement Award for poetry (USA 2010). In 2006, he founded the groundbreaking World Poetry Almanac. He has lived in Ulaanbaatar, the capital of Mongolia.

Arturo Dávila S.

ARTURO DÁVILA S. is the Chair of the Department of Modern Languages at Laney College, Oakland, and the founder of the Latinx Cultural Center. Dr. Dávila earned his doctorate in Romance Languages and Literatures at UC Berkeley, where he teaches a summer program in Mexican history and Nauatl language and culture. He specializes in colonial literature (Amerindian perspectives on the conquest of Mexico), contemporary Latin American, and Chicano literature. He has received four poetry awards: La ciudad dormida (Sor Juana Inés de la Cruz Prize, Mexico, 1995); Catulinarias (Antonio Machado Prize, Spain, 1998); Poemas para ser leídos en el metro (Juan Ramón Jiménez Prize, Spain, 2003); and La cuerda floja (Nicolás Guillén Prize, Caribbean Philosophical Association (CPA), 2016). He is the editor of the anthology, La Tinusa: Latin American Poets in the USA (2016). Current publications include Sátiras (2017), Tantos troncos truncos (2020), and También garganta el mar (2023). Professor Dávila's latest research project focuses on pre-Hispanic códices.

DOLORIO (3 Neo-baroque sonnets)

Jack Foley- In memoriam

I

NADA se puede más que ahora nunca
en lentas vibraciones laterales
barco fantasma en horizonte altivo
el alma en agua fría despeñando

Que todo se resume en esta vida
cuando en un grito equidistante al mar
sucumben transparentes cristalinas
venas de fuego hasta el final del día

Valor equinoccial en la batalla
que meridianos huesos ya se alejan
por despoblados cementerios calcios

Ardiente fósforo en desierto alumbra
el vuelo fulguroso hacia el olvido
que hay más vida en la muerte que en la vida

I

NOTHING can be done more than ever now
on slowly progressing lateral waves
phantom boat on a lofty horizon
the soul hurling itself into cold water

For everything is summed up in this life
when in a cry equidistant from the sea
transparent crystalline veins of fire
surrender to the day's last light.

Equinoctial courage in the battle
where meridian bones already drift
through vacant calcium graveyards

Where proud phosphorus silently glows
the dazzling flight towards oblivion
for there is more life in death than in this life

II

CALLA más boca en el silencio alondra
que mucho alumbra el que con fuego calla
habla del bien que en el presente estalla
pues la figura se estremece en sombras

Recuerda la firmeza de la talla
en pieles marchitadas que ahora escombran
del susto que no puede ni las nombra
que no hay más cuerpo firme en la batalla

Paisaje de recuerdos vagabundos
recorren la llanura estremecida
en terminantes tumbos y retumbos

Y ante esa fulminante fecha herida
recoge bien los frutos de este mundo
que vida hay en la muerte más que en vida

II

HUSH – there are more sounds in silence
for he who guards the secret fire glows the most
recall your goodness that is bursting forth
while your figure trembles in the shadows

Remember the firmness of your skin
withering and turning into rubble
from the fear that cannot be named
for no one can resist Death's final blow

Landscape of wandering memories
roaming across the trembling plain
in crashing stumbles and tumbles

And yet before the rapidly decaying day
gather the fruits of our fleeting world
for there is more life in death than in this life

III

DICHOSA MUERTE de mi bien tardío
palpitante furor de extremaunciones
oh campaneo en curvas de la glotis
sin siquiera saber de sus escalas

En cuestas delicadas estaciones
verano otoño primavera invierno
no hay troje más repleta que el vacío
en sentenciosos puertos peregrinos

Dejad ese rigor velad la pena
que negra más aún llega la muerte
de misteriosa luz enfebrecida

Salid al manantial del fuego eterno
en vuelo rectilíneo hacia el Misterio
más vida hay en la muerte que en la vida

III

BLESSED DEATH that we elude with fury
the dreaded performance of last rites
oh bells ringing in the quivering throat
without knowing their own musical scales

On delicate slopes the seasons
winter spring summer and fall
no granary is fuller than emptiness
in eerie desolate migrant ports

Forget the grief, veil the sorrow
for death always arrives on time
with its mysterious feverish light

Ascend to the spring of eternal fire
in straight flight towards the Unknown
for there is more life in death than in this life

(Translated by the author from the original in Spanish)

✷ ✷ ✷

Olchar E. Lindsann

Striking the Set

for Jack Foley,
Passed Into Text

⌣⌣⌣⌣⌣⌣⌣⌣⌣⌣⌣⌣⌣⌣⌣

"Jack Foley, where is he
In all these histories?"
– Jack, *The Ballad of Neglected Poets.*
ξξξξξξξξξξξξξξξξξξξξ
the final act
the fine old lack
is over *like that* –
on the poet curtly's
pulled the curtain
cold uncertain
vaudeville's maudlin
holy masque
boldly ask
showmen voided
hied for the nexTown

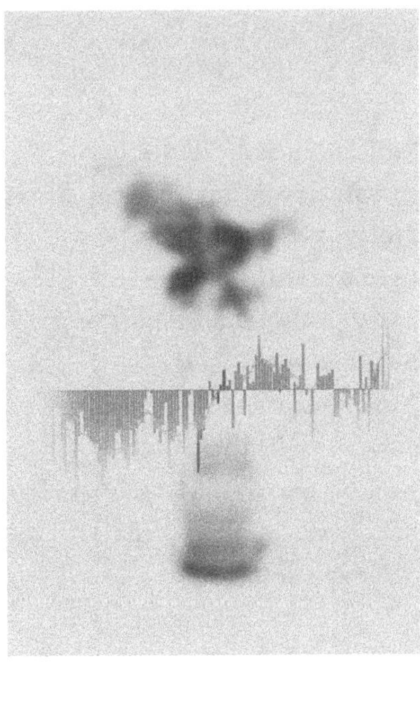

alive for the texTown
down in th'endless vale
sounding thinnest veil
yr voice its echo
regale Hades yr lyre
yr lyre its echo
regale Hades yr words
yr neWorlded brogue
regale Hades yr voice
ye singer of the fallen poets
singer, fallen poet
ye singer to the fallen poets
sing, fall poet
ye singer of forgotten poets
singer, forgotten poet
ye singer to forgotten poets
sing, for ten poets
ye our tribal mourner
we outrival all mourning
ye echo—verberate—rebound
yr cleaRich verses racket forth
from Death's radio-mawed vale
with foley-work immaculate
back same time to ~~morrow~~
wracked mainline for sorrow
on the Ether's Other side
Jack's name dies no more though
for showbiz never tires
no joke, no bit ever retires
nor history shake off yr words
yr poems ever on tour
on adepTongues of verse

Olchar E. Lindsann has published nearly 50 books and chapbooks of literature, theory, translation, and avant-garde history including six books of the ongoing series Arthur Dies (Luna Bisonte Prods), and most recently The Squitty Flange, an avant-garde twist on the nonsense poetry tradition. His poems have appeared in Otoliths, Lost & Found Times, Brave New Word, and elsewhere, his essays in No Quarter, Slova, & Fifth Estate; and he has performed sound poetry and lectured extensively. He is the editor of mOnocle-Lash Anti-Press, whose catalog includes over 250 print publications of the contemporary and historical avant-garde, and of the periodicals Rêvenance, Synapse, and The in-Appropriated Press. He translates work of the French avant-garde of the 19th & early 20th centuries.

in flashpot gilded halls
in rebirthing breath of print
in grimedank dives
ink rimed-pages' lives
in tattertorn tents
in th'leaves eternal re-turn
the show goes on
your show goes on
goes on
our show goes
go on
how

✷ ✷ ✷

Olchar E. Lindsann has published nearly 50 books and chapbooks of literature, theory, translation, and avant-garde history including six books of the ongoing series Arthur Dies (Luna Bisonte Prods), and most recently The Squitty Flange, an avant-garde twist on the nonsense poetry tradition. His poems have appeared in Otoliths, Lost & Found Times, Brave New Word, and elsewhere, his essays in No Quarter, Slova, & Fifth Estate; and he has performed sound poetry and lectured extensively. He is the editor of mOnocle-Lash Anti-Press, whose catalog includes over 250 print publications of the contemporary and historical avant-garde, and of the periodicals Rêvenance, Synapse, and The in-Appropriated Press. He translates work of the French avant-garde of the 19th & early 20th centuries.

Judy Grahn

Jack the Poet Laureate

Jack be nimble
Jack be quick
Jack the literary
thimblestick,
Jack the candle

I always thought we were both
Metal Dragons in Chinese astrology
born eleven days apart midsummer,
1940, born into the Civil Rights
Generation, born to make
connections, and tear worlds
open with words and steadfast
commitments to visions and actions.
every time I turned around
here's Jack, I wish to nominate
Poet Laureate of Oakland
of Berkeley, of San Francisco
of the South Bay
Poet Laureate of the Radio
of the Airways, Jack
Poet Laureate of Poet Hearts,

Jack Nimbletongue, turn around,
Jack's Poetry Newsletter, or
it's a reading, here's Jack,
it's an interview, Jack again,
it's my wedding, her's Jack
and Adele harmonizing their gift,
in my back yard, turn around,
it's a yearly tribute to Pat Parker,
Avotcja, here's Blackberri Poet,
me and here's Jack, Poet Laureate
of Tributes to other poets and
Jack Nimbleform, here's Cover to
Cover, Poet Laureate of Poetry's
Dialogues interstitched between lines
and spaces, here's
a memorial to the poet who flew
off a cliff. and here's Jack, here's Paul Mariah
reading his defiant poetry,
and Buddhist friends burning off
negativity and me crying under my hat
for privacy, and here's the beach where
they found her and here's friends
sending her ashes across the rough water
in a little burning boat,

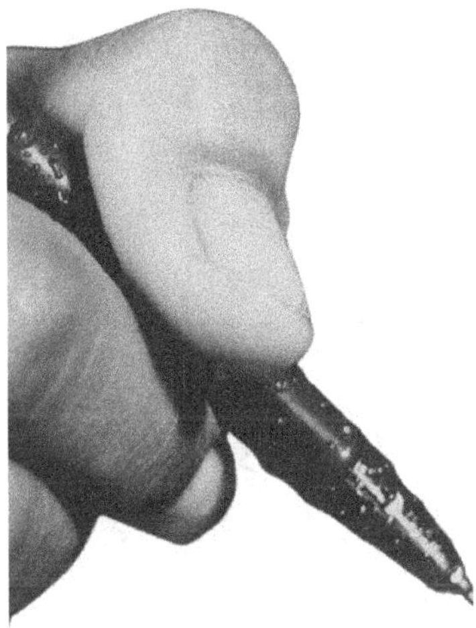

and I say to Jack, "She came to my house to complain
about how the men treated her."
"No, she came to my house to complain about how
the *women* treated her." And there we are
nose to nose and both right, with everything
wrong. And Jack, Poet Laureate of the Waves
of timc past, present and future, Jack
the Nimble, jumped the candle,

jumped the candlestick, jumped over
all of it. You are the Laureate, Jack.
May your work be read and appreciated
for a long, long time. May you know
how loved you are.

✷ ✷ ✷

Maw Shein Win

The Jook Joint

for Jack Foley, 2013

My buddy Jack wants
to show me his
favorite Chinese joint
in downtown Oakland.

I wonder if & secretly
hope it's my favorite
Chinese vegan joint
in Oakland Chinatown.

We spy a parking spot
out front of D & A,
smack on the corner
of Franklin & 7th.

Jack is ecstatic to show
off the menu, typed
up & plastered with
tape on the window.

My left eye starts to quiver,
pork intestines and blood noodles
chicken hearts on macaroni
beef tongue jook special

Uhm, where's the veggie?
I say & he says,
Come, come, now you must
see the inside!

Jack opens the door.
Beatific smile on his face,
he plucks two paper menus
from the hands of the host.

I scan the room.
Looks like the real thing,
no mustard-colored walls,
no cocktail specials.

Hey, this place looks
pretty great, I say,
then whisper, except for
the beef tongue jook.

* * *

Maw Shein Win's latest full-length poetry collection is Percussing the Thinking Jar (Omnidawn, 2024) which was shortlisted for the 2025 Northern California Book Award in Poetry. Her previous full-length collection Storage Unit for the Spirit House (Omnidawn, 2020) was longlisted for the PEN America 2021 Open Book Award and shortlisted for the Golden Poppy Award for Poetry. She is the inaugural poet laureate of El Cerrito, CA, the recipient of the 2025 Berkeley Poetry Festival Lifetime Achievement Award, and the 2025 Nomadic/SF Foundation Literary Award for Non-fiction. mawsheinwin.com

Judy Wells

Judy Wells' latest collection, Night at the Musée d'Orsay: Poems of Paris & Other Great European Cities, was published by Regent Press, 2023. Dear Phebe: The Dickinson Sisters Go West, poems about her Dickinson ancestors who traveled from Massachusetts to California in the 1860s, was published by Sugartown, 2018. Her Irish-themed poetry collections include The Glass Ship, Call Home, and Everything Irish. She lives in Berkeley.
www.judywellspoet.com

Dear Jack, St. Jacques, Frère Jacques,

Dear Jack, St. Jacques, Frère Jacques,
Irish-American friend, poet, brother—I've known you for so long from our 1980s days at the Coffee Mill in Oakland, California, reciting poems in a tiny space over the incessant noise of acoffee grinder, to your days as a KPFA radio personality presenting poetry to the world.
Thank you for your innovative poems, your love of Yeats, Mallarmé, vaudeville, radio, film,your poem about how the Irish became acceptable Americans through becoming film stars (not because they became cops, teachers, politicians!) and your love of Italian food (that extra plate of spaghetti you coaxed out of chefs to accompany your breakfast, your Italian heritage).
Thank you for writing blurbs for my three Irish-themed poetry books—Everything Irish, Call Home, and The Glass Ship. Thank you for your vulnerability in writing your beautiful Grief Songs about Adelle, your wife and poetry partner's death, poems for your new love Sangye, and even warning us in your last poems that you were an old man and dying yourself. We didn't want to believe you, but your poems told the truth.
Thank you for leading a brave, full creative life, collaborating with so many others along the way. Amen, Frère Jacques, I hope you're in heaven even though you didn't believe in it or at least in a place like "Tír na nÓg"—the Irish "Land of Youth" where there is no decay and you can still tap-dance to your "ditties." I miss you, Jack.

Judy Wells

* * *

"Babuji and Uncle on tour to Mars

Roshni Shajil (poet, artist, b. 2012)

Babuji and Uncle on tour to Mars.
In a rocket I colored in dreams,
Babuji's stories, I painted
Feeling his warmth.
Uncle's poems, I painted
Feeling his fondness and love
K M Anthru, with tales that shine,
Jack Foley, poet from Oakland
At eighty-five, his verses still strong.
Both are my guiding stars.
On Mars, they light the dark.
Together they dance
Tap, tap, tap
I see the duo dance.
Babuji, your kindness moves my brush,
Uncle, your words give me strength.
Our bond will not part,
You both are in my heart.

Uncle, you are 85
And I am 8 + 5 =13
So, you are 13
Happy birthday, Uncle.

Love, Love, Love

ack Foley and his mother, 1945.
Perhaps in New Jersey.

This is my son
Ain't he
something?

and I wrote...

Darkness
Give way to the sunlit;
Huge moon
Bow before him;
to seek blessings
of a life lavish
of historical moments;
Shadows and lights
Uncertain though,
Learnt their meaning.

He is young
Here, he is to teach
how age makes us
grow young.

To be with him
Is like to be with light
To be with him
Is to be with
A sunlit moon and
A poetry lit sun

-Shajil Anthru

As you once said,,
you are now in Mars
amd we are to explore you
through your writings

Jack, There is no end ...

* * *

Worship while in limelight
Ignore if in oblivion
Overlook when departed
is the destiny
of a litterateur or artist.

-K M Anthru in his book
"Prathibhadarshanam"

For Jack Foley, Still Illuminating the World

Lantern Walking Ahead

ISBN : 978-81-988393-5-0

Jack Foley as the Synonym to Creativity and also as the Unquestioning master at Poetry
------Shajil Anthru

A collection of tribute poems for Jack Foley

Editor

Shajil Anthru

A Real Magazine Production

www.ingramcontent.com/pod-product-compliance
Lightning Source LLC
Chambersburg PA
CBHW062147160726
48282CB00027B/957
* 9 7 8 8 1 9 8 8 3 9 3 5 0 *